Kate was a Highland dancer.
She took classes each week,
So she could learn
The proper technique.

She learned to:

Turn out and point,   High cut and leap,

Kate's teacher thought she was ready
For a new challenge to try.
She said, "You should compete
At the Highland Games in July."

Kate liked the idea.
That sounded fun!
She'd wear her kilt, blouse and vest,
And her hair in a bun.

"BUT," her teacher warned...

"You have to practice at home,
So you'll be prepared
To dance your best
When you get there."

Kate promised she would.
Then she discovered
That dancing at home
Wasn't as fun without others.

In her room she danced:

Point, back, toe and shake,
Rock, two, three, four.
Point, back, toe and shake,
Rock, two, three, four.

Point, back, toe and shake,
Rock, two, three, four...
Kate stopped. She was done.
She didn't want to practice anymore.

As the Highland Games got closer,
Her teacher was encouraging.
"Practice makes perfect," she said,
But Kate didn't do anything.

Her mom asked, "Why don't you try
Just a few minutes each day?"
"No, I'm good enough," Kate said.
"I'm going outside to play."

Fast forward to July
To the day of the Games,
Kate registered, got her number,
Then waited to go onstage.

The first dance was the fling
(Which went fine),
And when she was done
Kate said, "I didn't have to practice.
I told you, Mom."

But next was the sword dance,
Which is a lot more tricky.
Although she started out okay,
It went downhill quickly...

First her toe touched the blade—
Just a tiny tap, a wee *ting*—
So maybe the judge
Didn't notice a thing.

Kate kept on going.
Then the music got faster.
That's when it happened:

BIG DISASTER!

Kate kicked the sword hard.
The *CLANKETY-CLANK* was so loud
A collective gasp
Came from the crowd.

The sword slid down the floor
To where the piper played.
It hit him in the ankles
And knocked him off the stage.

He fell forward
And landed on the ground,
Bagpipes first—
Oh, what a sound!

MEANWHILE...

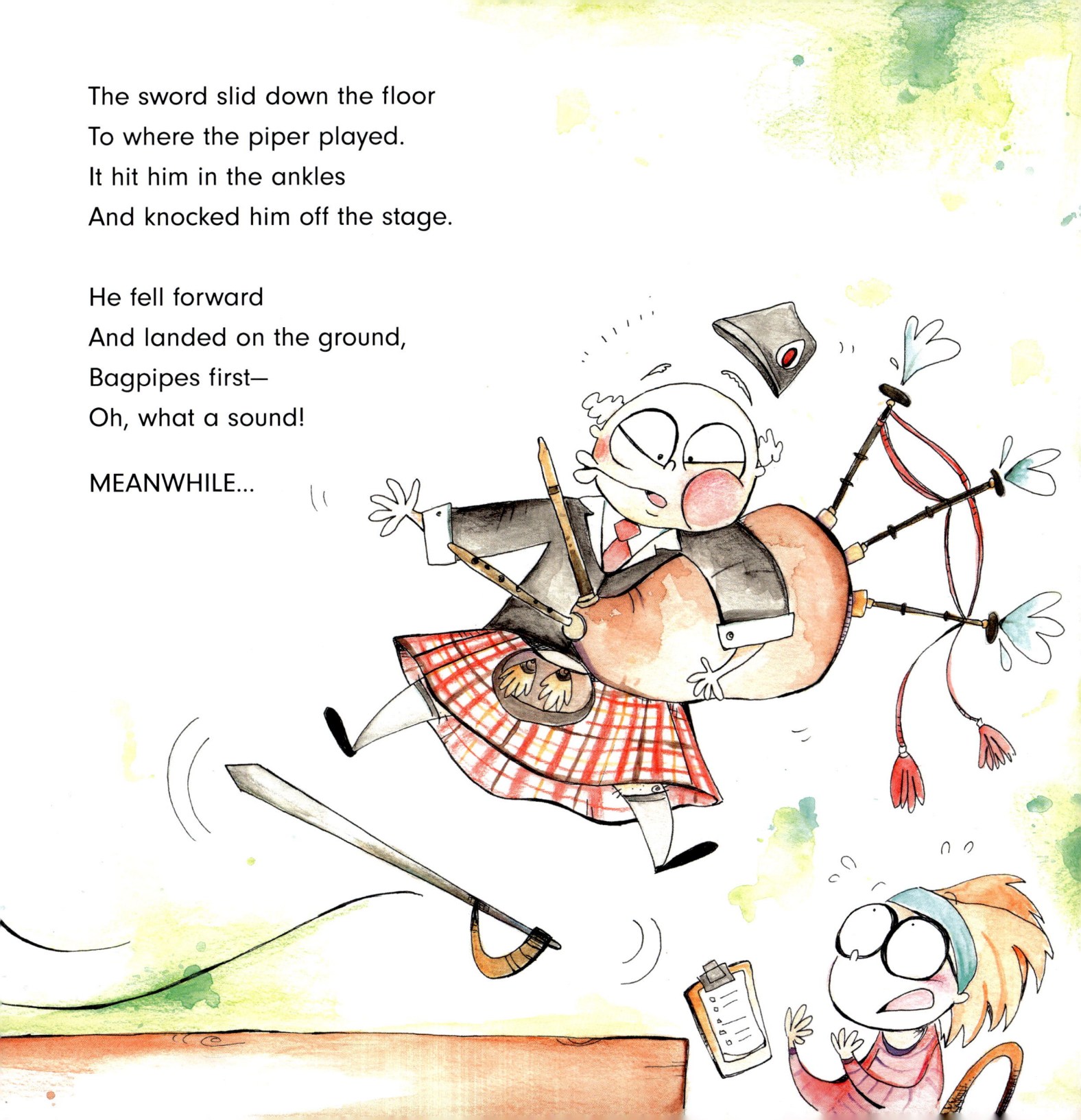

The heavy events were near the Highland dance tent
And it was time for the caber toss.
A competitor was getting ready,
Trying to keep the pole steady...

But the squished bagpipes squawking
Startled him so,
He lost his balance
Before he could throw.

The caber tipped
And he wasn't able
To keep it from crashing
Into the big awards table.

The weight of it landing
(Thankfully where no one was standing),
Launched a trophy into the air.
It went up so high—OH MY, OH MY!
Everyone stopped and stared.

It soared...

Over the genealogy table
And the first aid station,

Above the fiddling workshop
And the wool spinning demonstration.

It started downward
At the Celtic music tent, Bounced on the roof
Then away it went.

The trophy flew to where
A pipe band was performing,
And landed on the bass drummer
Without any warning.

It came down on her head
Just like a hat.
Still she kept on *BOOM-BOOMING*
With the snare drummers' *rat-a-tat-tat*.

But she couldn't see
Because it covered her eyes.
She tried to shake it off.
Then to her surprise,

Instead, her big drum
Detached from her chest.
And rolled away! (OH NO!)
Are you ready for the rest?

Okay. So:

The drum knocked open the gate
Where sheep for the herding demonstration grazed.

And at first they seemed completely unfazed.

But soon they took advantage
Of their chance to be free,
And the whole herd ran out
Quite happily.

The lambs and ewes
Really moved their hooves.
And quickly made their way
To the vendors' booths.

The kiltmakers were at
The end of a row
So when the sheep tipped their tent,
The rest fell like dominoes.

Next the souvenir booth collapsed,
Then the store display for All Things Scottish.
You get the idea—
It was completely demolished.

The sheep kept on going,
And things went from *baa, baa,* baaaad to worse.
They trampled the kids' zone
And wrecked the mini golf course.

They ran through the picnic area
Past the baker selling scones.
They made it to the Highland dance tent
Where Kate stood in shock, alone.

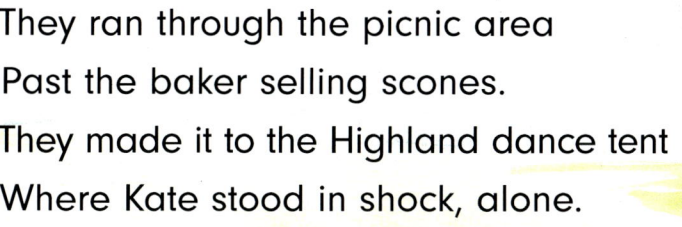

She watched a sheep trip
And pull a tent peg out.
It was a scary situation,
There was no doubt.

The tent's roof started to sag,
First one side, then the other.

"Help! Help! Help!"
Kate called for her mother.

The next two seconds
Were all quite a blur,
As the tent came down
Right on top of her.

But Kate wasn't hurt.
She really was fine.
Except now she was sure
She'd practice next time.